Dear Miss Lorraine
& Jani

All is
Witn
God in the Uni

FLAPPY

AND THE ANIMALS

FLAPPY

AND THE ANIMALS

BY JULIETTE MCNULTY

Rutledge Books, Inc.
8 F.J. Clarke Circle, Bethel, CT 06801

Manufactured in the United States of America

Library of Congress Cataloging in Publication Data
McNulty, Juliette
Flappy and the animals/Juliette McNulty.
p.   cm.
ISBN 1-88750-12-6

I. Farm life--Juvenile Fiction. 2. Domestic animals--Juvenile
fiction I. Title. (1. Farm life--Fiction. 2. Domestic animals--Fiction.
I. Title)
(E) -- dc20   95–72384

TO MY DAUGHTER, WHITNEY
WHO LOVES ANIMALS

A long time ago, in the village of Townville, lived a young boy named Flappy and his father, Flannel.

They lived with their cow Mo, Bo the bull, Maude the hen, Korba the rooster, Ramzie the sheep, Franzie the goat, and their dog Bushy.

Flappy had been his father's companion since the day he was born. "Ma is in Heaven with the Lord," said Flappy to Bushy, as he rubbed Bushy's head with his rough little fingers.

"Woof! Woof!" barked Bushy. He always seemed to understand his little friend.

Flappy continued, "Pa said that one day we will all go to Heaven to be with Ma. And we'll all be a family again. Wouldn't it be nice to see Ma, Bushy? Wouldn't it? Wouldn't it?"

Bushy shook his head. "Woof! Woof!" Flappy wiggled Bushy's long brown ears, gave him a big hug, and said laughingly, "I knew you would like that."

Just then, Flannel walked out of the old broken down kitchen onto the front porch and said, "Hey, son, it's time to milk the cow. Mo doesn't like to be kept waiting, you know. Her teats get very hot when they're full and she looks forward to having someone squeeze the milk out of them." Flappy answered, "Okay Pa, I'm on my way." Not one minute passed before Flappy walked to the barn wearing his faded blue overalls, his red-striped cotton shirt, his brown leather boots that went all the way up to his knees, a straw hat on his dark brown hair, and a navy blue polka dot scarf around his neck.

He opened the gray wooden gate and walked to the barn. Once there, he reached over to the old wooden table on the left side of the open gate and picked up the aluminum milking bucket.

Underneath the table was a small wooden stool. Flappy bent down, picked up the stool and set it down on the hay and mud left by the rain the night before.

Flappy gave Mo a gentle pat on the back and said, "All right girl... I didn't mean to keep you waiting. I'll be very gentle. I promise."

Mo reassured Flappy that she forgave him with a big, **"MOO! MOO!"**

Flappy sat down on the wooden stool. With a gentle pull..then another..and a squeeze of Mo's blown-up teats a flow of white delicious milk began to squirt out from Mo's teats into the milking bucket.

After Flappy finished milking Mo, he got up from the stool, jumped up as high as he could, and exclaimed joyfully,

"Ya...Hoo! We did it girl!" He always said that whenever he finished milking Mo.

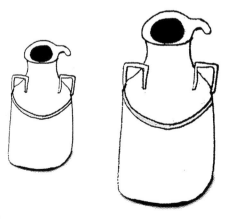

Flappy grasped the handle of the bucket of milk and slid it gently to the side, away from Mo's hind legs. He turned to his Pa who was still standing on the porch watching him from afar and said, "It's mighty nice to let her know that she's done a great job, you know." Flappy often said that to his Pa.

Flannel proudly replied, "You're right, son! We should show her how much we appreciate her giving us her milk to drink and sell to other folks in town, so we can buy enough food to eat."

Suddenly, Flappy turned around and faced Mo. He threw his hat up in the air and shouted, "Hee...Haw! Ya...Hoo!" He kicked his heels together and did the cowboy dance.

Flappy clapped his little hands cheerfully while singing this song:

I'm happy, I'm happy
Hee-Haw, Hee-Haw.
I'm happy, I'm happy
Hee-Haw, Hee-Haw
Ya...Hoo!

When Mo heard Flappy singing and clapping, she was so happy that she decided to join in. She began to move her left hind leg, then the right hind leg, then the left front leg, and the right front leg while shaking her head, flapping her ears. Before you know it...Mo was dancing too!

Not long after, Bo, who was standing on the other side of the barn watching the whole scene while chewing on a pile of crispy hay, decided to join in the fun as well. He moved his front legs up and down, as if he were doing the galloping dance.

Korba was behind the bamboo dog house, crunching on some leftover corn from the day before, and heard the commotion coming from the barn. Suddenly...he stopped. He looked up in the blue sky above him and thought to himself, "Hum...it sounds like there is a party going on over there. It wouldn't hurt to take a look."

As Korba walked closer to the gray wooden gate, the sounds of singing, hands clapping, and laughter seemed louder and louder. So he decided to go inside. When he entered the barn, he couldn't believe his tiny biddy eyes. Flappy, Mo, and Bo, were having a ball.

Korba streeeeeetched out his red feathered wings. He made a small jump, then a higher jump, then another, and by the time everybody asked, "Would you like to join in?" Korba was already dancing.

Meanwhile, Maude, whose eggs had just hatched a week earlier, was standing by the apple tree, digging some worms to feed her baby chicks. She heard the laughter and the singing too.

Maude gave each of her little chicks a long juicy worm for lunch and after they ate it, she said, "Come on children! Let's go and see what has gotten everybody so heated up at this time of the day!"

The six little chicks with soft yellow feathers followed their mother joyfully to where the noise was coming from. When they got inside the barn, Maude said to her little chicks, "All right children, listen up! Today, you're going to have your very first dancing lesson."

All the chicks replied harmoniously, "DANCING LESSON! What is that, Mommy?"

Maude answered smilingly, "It is an exercise you do with your body that makes you very happy, strong, and healthy. Now watch me very carefully and do what I do."

"Okay!" replied the chorus. Maude put her little chicks in a circle and stood in the middle of it. She said to them, "Now stretch your wings." Then..."Easy now kids. Your wings are very fragile you know and your little bones aren't strong enough, so don't hurt yourselves."

The little chicks streeeeeetched their tiny wings gaily. Maude continued, "Now jump up and down, but not too high, so when you land on the ground, you won't break a bone."

The chicks jumped up and down, and up and down. "That's it! You've got it!" said Maude proudly to her little chicks, as they were all doing the cowboy dance.

Meanwhile, Ramzy, Franzie, and Bushy were in the garden with Flannel, harvesting some red plump tomatoes to sell to the local food store when suddenly...Bushy began to bark, "Woof! Woof!" The noise had reached his long brown ears.

"What is it, Bushy?" asked Flannel. "Did you see something?" Bushy continued to bark, "Woof, Woof! Woof, Woof!" while running in the direction of the noise.

"Wait for me!" yelled Flannel, putting down the basket full of red tomatoes on the wet ground. He ran after Bushy. "Hey Bushy, stop! Wait for me!" continued Flannel, but Bushy kept on running faster and faster as if he were being chased by a giant lion.

When Bushy finally stopped by the gray wooden gate in front of the barn, Flannel was out of breath. He gasped.."Bushy..Huh..Huh..Huh.." He said, "What is the matter?" Without saying a word, Bushy ran inside the barn. Flannel followed him. Behind Flannel Ramzy and Franzie came running.

Everybody was still dancing happily inside the barn. Bushy looked around and said, "What in a dog's name is going on here?"

"We're doing the cowboy dance, come on and join us," answered Bo.

"Cowboy dance! Wait a minute. I don't know how to dance, so how can I join in the fun?" replied Bushy. Both Ramzy and Franzie answered, "Don't worry, we'll teach you."

Ramzy and Franzie began to kick their legs, and Bushy kicked his legs too. Then he shook his long brown ears, wagged his curly tail, and before you know it, Bushy was dancing too. Just then..."Hold everything everybody!" exclaimed Flannel with his hands up. "I forgot something."

"What is it Pa?" asked Flappy. "I'll be right back, " replied Flannel. He ran to the front porch, into the broken down kitchen, and opened the door to the cupboard. He stuck his large hands all the way in the back of the top shelf and pulled out an old rusty harmonica.

Flannel had not played his harmonica in eight years. He had been working so hard in the garden, and the barn, and taking care of his son, that he hardly had any time for fun.

Flannel blew the dust out of the old harmonica, wiped the rust off with his dark green cotton shirt, and began playing his instrument while dancing all the way back to the barn. When they heard the music, the whole gang started to dance again.

Flannel, Flappy, Maude and her little chicks, Mo, Bo, Ramzy, Franzie, Korba, and Bushy were all doing the cowboy dance while Flannel played his old harmonica, and Flappy sang his song:

I'm happy, I'm happy
Hee-Haw, Hee-Haw.
I'm happy, I'm happy
YA...HOO!

"One more time!" shouted Flappy laughingly, and the whole gang sang happily together.

Since that day, life for Flappy, Flannel, and their animals was always joyful.